The Ca
Garden Monster

by Nancy Bentley

Illustrated by Hector Borlasca

SCHOLASTIC INC.

NEW YORK TORONTO LONDON AUCKLAND SYDNEY
MEXICO CITY NEW DELHI HONG KONG BUENOS AIRES

To John,
my favorite garden monster
—N.B.

To my father, Hector
—H.B.

ISBN 0-439-47470-1

12 11 10 9 8 7 6 5 4 3 2 1 3 4 5 6 7 8/0

Printed in the U.S.A.
First printing, March 2003 23

Book design by Jennifer Rinaldi Windau

CHAPTER 1

Nick Anderson's clubhouse door stood open.

"Who's in there?" he called. Nobody answered. Bread crumbs were on the floor. A peanut-butter-and-jelly jar lay under the table. Footprints covered the floor.

"That's the second time someone broke into our clubhouse," Nick said. "This time they got a free lunch."

He wrote KEEP OUT on a sign and nailed it to the door.

His sister, Rachel, came running.

"There's a monster out there! A monster!"

"What are you talking about?" Nick asked.

"There's a garden monster around our house!" Rachel cried. "I can prove it."

She pointed to the flower bed. All the pansies lay facedown."Every stem is broken. And look! Garden monster tracks!"

Nick got down on his hands and knees. "It could be Jake, the cat."

Then Nick saw more tracks. Some were small and round. Some looked like little hands. Some looked like little feet.

Rachel sniffled. "I'm having a tea party tomorrow with Shelly and Bitsy. I won't have one pansy to show them."

Nick walked around the backyard. Maybe Rachel was right. There were tracks all over the place. Tracks in the flower beds. Tracks near his clubhouse. What if her garden monster had also broken into his clubhouse?

"Let's talk this over," Nick said. He could see it was time for the Nature Investigators to find out who or what the garden monster was.

CHAPTER 2

At lunch, Nick pulled out his Nature Investigator notebook. "Let's write down what happened." He put a large number 1 on a clean sheet of paper.

"First, someone broke into my clubhouse two times."

"It could have been the wind," Rachel said.

Nick cupped his chin in his hand. "How could the wind scratch the door?"

He wrote down the number 2. "Then someone ate my peanut butter and jelly." It was his favorite spread.

"Maybe it was Manny," Rachel said. "Remember how mad he was when you and Kyle didn't invite him to lunch?"

Kyle was Nick's best friend. Manny was his little brother.

"Manny is too young to play with Kyle and me," Nick said. Would Manny wreck their lunch?

"Don't forget the most important crime," said Rachel. "Number three. Stepping on my pansies."

Nick scratched his head. Someone was sneaking around the yard, all right. But who was it? He drew a long line down the middle of another page. He wrote CLUES on one side and SUSPECTS on the other.

Under CLUES he wrote: *clubhouse door, peanut butter and jelly, broken pansies*, and *tracks.* Under SUSPECTS he wrote: *wind, Jake*, and *Manny.*

"Let's look at those tracks again," Nick said.

A gentle rushing sound outside made Nick and Rachel look at each other.

"Did Dad fix the sprinkler system?" Rachel asked.

"Oh, no!" Nick's face became pale. "There goes our evidence!"

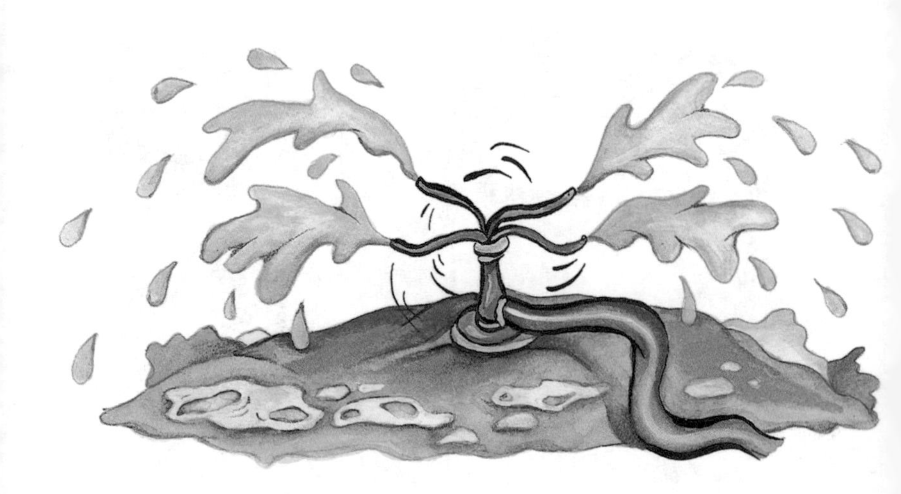

CHAPTER 3

The sprinklers stopped. But the tracks were gone. All Nick could see were puddles.

"Let's keep looking," he said. "Maybe Dad's sprinklers didn't get everything."

But the sprinkler system had worked well. Nick and Rachel could not find one track.

Rachel decided to get ready for her tea party. "I'll use vegetables instead." She looked proudly at her radishes and beans.

Nick stayed at the picnic table. He tried to remember what the tracks looked like.

"Rachel, I have an idea," he said. "Let's ask Mom if we can sleep outside in our tent tonight. Then we can see who's coming to our backyard!"

"Outside?" Rachel asked. "In the dark?"

It was one thing to find monster tracks. It was another thing to spend the night in monster territory.

CHAPTER 4

Mom agreed to let Nick and Rachel sleep in the tent. "Don't forget your flashlights," she said. "Just in case you come back."

"I'm not coming back into the house," Nick said. There was a nature mystery in his backyard. And he was going to solve it.

Rachel carried five dolls plus Wilhelm, her big teddy bear, into the tent.

"With that bear there's not enough room for me and my sleeping bag in here!" Nick said.

Rachel held her teddy bear around its stomach.

Buzzzzz. Something buzzed in Nick's ear.

He grabbed his pillow.

"Hey! Stop hitting Wilhelm!" Rachel cried out.

"I'm not hitting Wilhelm. I'm swatting mosquitoes!"

Suddenly, Nick heard a crack in the backyard.

Nick grabbed the big teddy bear and held on tight.

They heard a soft meow outside.

"Jake!" Nick whispered.

Soon Rachel fell asleep. Then Nick heard another crunch. It was close to the vegetable garden. He didn't want to wake Rachel. But he didn't want to go outside by himself.

Nick stuck his head out of the tent and turned on his flashlight. Bright yellow eyes stared back at him.

Nick pulled back inside the tent. He slid down into his sleeping bag. He lay there a long time, holding his breath.

Nothing outside made a noise. But Nick was wide-awake. He hadn't seen two yellow eyes. He'd seen four. There wasn't just one monster in their garden—there were two!

CHAPTER 5

Nick heard a noise outside the tent. He wiped the sleep out of his eyes.

Rachel stood by the vegetable garden—or what was left of it. Half of the cornstalks had been broken off. Rachel walked closer.

"STOP!" Nick shouted. "Don't walk there!"

He stared at the footprints. Some of them looked like little feet and hands.

"Maybe Manny walked around while we were asleep," Rachel said.

Nick looked at his sister. "I saw the garden monster last night."

Rachel gasped. "Why didn't you wake me?" She put her hands on her hips. "I'm supposed to be your partner!"

Nick looked away. "Well, I didn't exactly see *him*. I saw *them*. I saw two sets of eyes."

Rachel pulled out her drawing pad. The tracks near the corn were clear to see. She drew as many as she could.

"What do we do next?" she asked.

"Let's see if the tracks can help us find our garden monsters!" Nick answered.

CHAPTER 6

All day, Nick looked at Rachel's drawings and thought about the garden monsters. Kyle came over and examined the scratches on the clubhouse door. "They sure have sharp claws."

"I think I know who they are, but I've got to prove it," Nick said.

"How are you going to do that?" Kyle asked.

"Tonight, I'm putting our garbage can against the clubhouse door," Nick said. "When the garden monsters try to open the door, we'll catch them in the act."

That night, Nick and Rachel planned to sleep in the tent again. This time, Nick brought mosquito repellent.

Rachel carried only one doll.

Nick brought along a couple of saucepan lids.

Right after the sun went down, they heard sounds from the garden.

"What's that?" Rachel whispered.

A soft meow came from under a bush.

"Jake," Nick said. They both laughed. Soon they fell asleep.

A loud crash near the clubhouse woke them up.

Rachel grabbed Nick's arm. "Someone knocked over the garbage can!"

"Shhh!" Nick unzipped the tent and grabbed Rachel's hand. It was shaking.

Something was pushing and shoving the garbage can.

"Maybe it's a bear!" Rachel said.

"I think it's something else. On the count of three, turn on your flashlight!" Nick commanded. "One, two, *three*!" In front of the clubhouse door stood two furry garden monsters.

CHAPTER 7

"Just as I thought," Nick said. "Raccoons! Bears don't have tails like that." He pointed to two long black-and-yellowish-white ringed tails.

"They have masks on!" Rachel screamed.

"Raccoons always wear masks," Nick said.

A large raccoon pushed the garbage can with its front paws. Next to the large one was a smaller raccoon.

"Leave our garden alone!" Nick and Rachel banged the saucepan lids together.

Both raccoons jumped away from the garbage can and ran off.

"How did you guess they were raccoons?" Rachel asked.

Nick took off his Nature Investigator hat. "The wind couldn't leave muddy marks on the clubhouse floor."

"Manny could have made the footprints," Rachel said.

"But Manny always wears his shoes," Nick said. "And he wouldn't scratch the door like that."

"Jake can scratch," Rachel said.

"But he couldn't open the jar."

“What made you so *sure*?” Rachel asked.

“You did.” He pulled Rachel’s drawing from his back pocket. “Their tracks look just like little hands! Also, raccoons come out at night. That’s when we saw them.”

Rachel paused. "How do we *keep* them out of our garden?"

"Dad fixed the sprinkler system. Let's ask him to put up a fence," Nick said. "And Kyle and I will have to be more careful about our food."

Rachel gave her brother a big hug. "You're the best Nature Investigator I know!"

"And you're the best partner a Nature Investigator could have," Nick said.

The next day, Rachel had her tea party with Shelly and Bitsy. She drew a menu that said First Annual Garden Monster Tea Party. She made lemonade, iced tea, and raccoon cupcakes.

Nick posted a big sign that said GARDEN MONSTER—CASE CLOSED.

RACCOON FACTS

What do they look like?

- Brownish-gray bodies
- Humped back
- Two to three feet long
- Black-and-white "bandit" face mask
- Weigh between ten and forty pounds
- Bushy tail with black-and-yellowish-white rings
- Five toes on all four feet

Where do they live?

- In wooded areas
- Near clean water

What do they eat?

- Bird eggs, young animals, greens, nuts, insects, and berries
- People's leftovers and garbage — almost anything!

Female raccoons give birth, from April to June, to an average litter of three or four babies.

Tracks

CAT

HUMAN

RACCOON